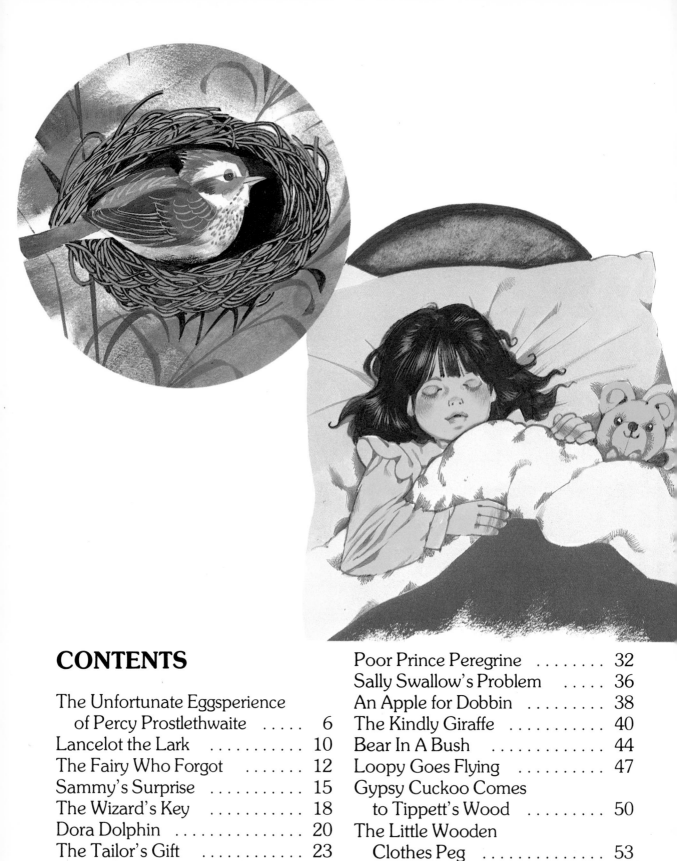

CONTENTS

The Unfortunate Eggsperience
   of Percy Prostlethwaite 6
Lancelot the Lark 10
The Fairy Who Forgot 12
Sammy's Surprise 15
The Wizard's Key 18
Dora Dolphin 20
The Tailor's Gift 23
Night and Day 26
The Dragon Who Caught
   A Cold 28

Poor Prince Peregrine 32
Sally Swallow's Problem 36
An Apple for Dobbin 38
The Kindly Giraffe 40
Bear In A Bush 44
Loopy Goes Flying 47
Gypsy Cuckoo Comes
   to Tippett's Wood 50
The Little Wooden
   Clothes Peg 53
Wise Old World 56
The Naughty Calf 58
Clovis Kitten's First Christmas . 60

Three~Minute Bedtime Stories

Published 1985 by Derrydale Books,
Distributed by Crown Publishers, Inc.

Derrydale Books
New York

The Unfortunate Eggsperience of Percy Prostlethwaite

by Norman Leaver

Percy Prostlethwaite always ate six boiled eggs for breakfast. Well, not always; sometimes he had eight, or even ten. And then again, on Saturdays and Sundays he had six *fried* eggs, with bacon, and tomatoes, and fried bread, and beans, and toast. But his tea only had *five* spoons of sugar in it . . .

Percy Prostlethwaite would have his six, or eight, or ten boiled eggs all in a row, each in its own egg cup, and he would eat them slowly, one at a time. He would put the first egg, in its egg cup, in front of him, then he would pick up his spoon and tap the top of the egg, first in the centre, and then all around the top, until it was nicely broken. Then he would pick off all the bits of eggshell and put them carefully on a plate. Then he would dig his spoon into the egg white, carefully lift up a spoonful of egg, which he would put on one side for later, and there would be the yolk, all soft and golden, just the way he liked it.

Percy Prostlethwaite always ate the yolk first. He would pick up a piece of toast, nice and crisp, with lashings of

butter on it, cut to just the right width to go into the egg. He would plunge it into the yolk, and then start eating.

Every morning at breakfast time, Mrs Prostlethwaite, Percy's mother, would say, just as Percy was eating his first egg, "Ee, Percy, one of these days you're going to get egg bound."

Percy never said anything, he would just keep munching, and think, "Rubbish!"

By about his fourth egg, Mr Prostlethwaite, Percy's father, would come in for his breakfast, and would say, "Ee, Percy, you're going to get egg bound one of these days."

Percy wouldn't say anything, he would just keep munching, and think, "Rubbish!" again.

Now, by the time Percy had his tenth birthday, it was estimated that he had eaten something like twenty-nine thousand two hundred and forty-six eggs. And what with eating five school dinners a day, because four of his friends didn't like theirs, not to mention a big meal at night, plus a few bags of crisps and bars of chocolate — just to keep him from fading away between

meals — he was getting rather large,
in fact he was huge,
in actual fact, and to be quite truthful, he was MASSIVE.

He was only four feet six inches tall, but he was *five* feet six inches round the middle.

His head went straight down to his shoulders, his neck having disappeared when he was four. His shoulders went straight out to his waist, and then he started getting narrower again until he came to his feet.

A special treat was waiting for him when he got up. There, for his birthday present, was his very own frying pan, three feet wide, and a book entitled *1001 Ways to Make an Omelette*. Knowing Percy, he would probably make all 1001 at the same time. Reading the omelette book gave him quite an appetite, so when he went down to breakfast he had *twenty-five boiled eggs*, which was a record even for him.

After breakfast, Percy's father told

him that they were all going to the seaside for the day, so they gathered their towels and swimming trunks and things, and off they went in their truck, which they had to have to carry Percy from place to place.

It was great at the seaside. Mrs Prostlethwaite laid out the blanket for Percy to sit on, while Mr Prostlethwaite went to get two deck chairs. Percy got into the back of the truck and changed into his swimming trunks, which is not easy when you can't bend over. But with a lot of grunting and puffing he finally made it, then he lay down on the blanket.

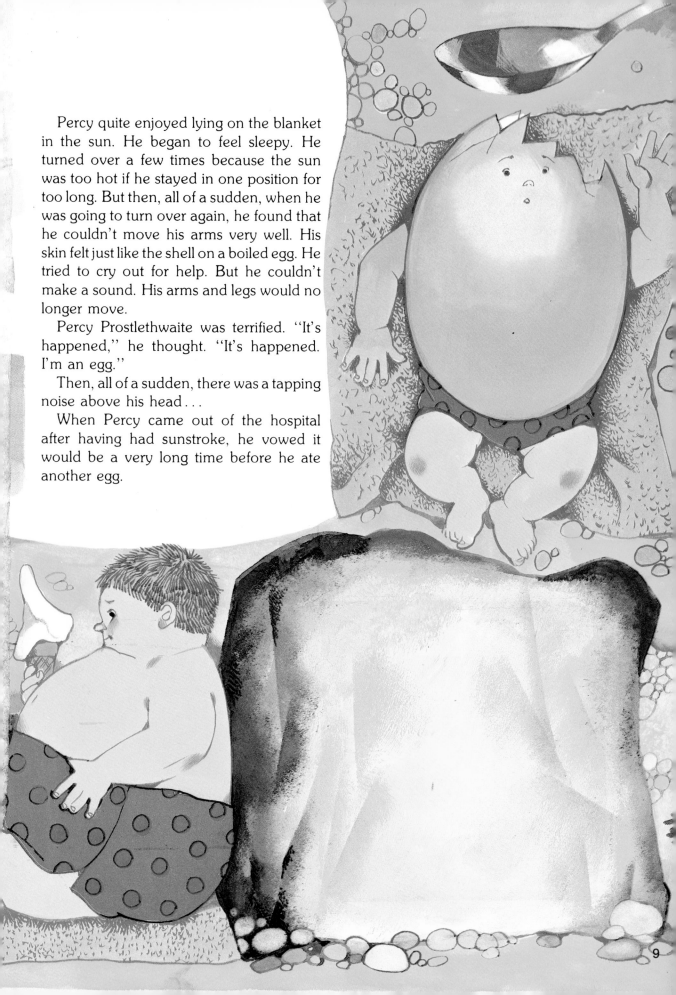

Percy quite enjoyed lying on the blanket in the sun. He began to feel sleepy. He turned over a few times because the sun was too hot if he stayed in one position for too long. But then, all of a sudden, when he was going to turn over again, he found that he couldn't move his arms very well. His skin felt just like the shell on a boiled egg. He tried to cry out for help. But he couldn't make a sound. His arms and legs would no longer move.

Percy Prostlethwaite was terrified. "It's happened," he thought. "It's happened. I'm an egg."

Then, all of a sudden, there was a tapping noise above his head . . .

When Percy came out of the hospital after having had sunstroke, he vowed it would be a very long time before he ate another egg.

Lancelot the Lark

by Moira Stubley

In the grassy woodland glade Marmaduke the Magpie was just opening one eye on the new day. What a glorious day it was. Sunshine was glancing through the trees. Marmaduke stirred in his cosy nest and opened the other eye. He peered into the next tree where his friends the Larks nested. "Oh, dear me," he sighed, "young Lancelot is still in bed!"

At that moment, a loud fluttering of wings and the glorious song of a dozen larks filled the glade. Since early daybreak the larks had been flying high above the clouds making beautiful music to welcome the dawn. But not young Lancelot. He never stirred until half-past nine. Nothing seemed to wake him . . . he just slept and slept!

"Still in his nest, I suppose," trilled Mother Lark as she passed Marmaduke's tree. "What a disgrace that boy is." His brothers and sisters and cousins giggled and

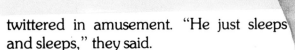

twittered in amusement. "He just sleeps and sleeps," they said.

Their laughter roused the sleepy Lancelot. Stretching his wings and opening his eyes he woke to greet the sunshine with a great big yawn. As he saw the other larks watching him he dived back into the nest and hid his sleepy face. Oh dear. He was late again. Why could he never wake up on time? He felt so ashamed.

"Lancelot," called Marmaduke, and a tiny head peeped over the nest.

"Oh, Marmaduke, what am I to do? The others hardly speak to me now and I am so ashamed. Can you help me, Marmaduke?"

"Well, young Lancelot, I shall give it some thought," answered Marmaduke.

Marmaduke was as good as his word. He thought. He consulted the animals, the insects and finally the flowers. That was when he had a bright idea.

Marmaduke arrived home that evening in great excitement. "Hurry up, young Lancelot," he called. "Pack all your things. You're moving house."

"M . .m . .moving house?" Lancelot stammered. "But all the larks live here in the glade."

"Do you want my help or not?" demanded Marmaduke.

"Oh yes, Marmaduke, of course I do," said Lancelot, and set about gathering together all his belongings.

Soon they had him well settled in a tree right on the edge of the wood. "There," said Marmaduke proudly, "that's perfect!"

"I don't want to seem ungrateful," Lancelot began, "but it's really very much like the tree I've just left."

"Ah, yes! But look down below," said Marmaduke in triumph. Covering the grass like a blue and lilac carpet were hundreds of bluebells and harebells. "I've had a word with them," Marmaduke explained, "and every flower has agreed to tinkle its bell as loudly as it can, to waken you up each morning. It's no trouble to them; that's why they have bells. They're very pleased to help."

Lancelot was so delighted that he leapt two feet in the air, right out of the tree, turned a somersault and landed upside down on the branch. The flowers below, seeing his antics, tinkled their bells in amusement. As he heard the lovely sound, Lancelot gasped in delight. "Oh, thank you, bluebells. Thank you, harebells," he chirped. "Tomorrow I shall sing my heart out to welcome the dawn."

THE FAIRY WHO FORGOT

by Dorothy Whybrow

Fairy Harebell was in disgrace. No one in Fairyland would talk to her.

Last night she had been given a very important job to do. And she had forgotten!

"We are all very disappointed in you," said the Fairy Queen sternly. "You have made a little girl very miserable — and that is unforgiveable!"

Harebell hung her head in shame and two big tears trickled down her cheeks. How could she have forgotten? Yesterday, Suzy Adams's first tooth had come out, when she was biting an apple. She had put it under her pillow when she went to bed. Fairy Harebell had been chosen to collect it and to leave a shiny silver **quarter** in its place.

"Why did you forget?" asked the Fairy Queen.

Harebell explained that she had been so excited to be chosen out of all the fairies, that she had set off early, with the bright **quarter** tucked carefully into the pocket of her blue dress. But on the way she had met Fairy Snowdrop, who was crying because she had caught her green ribbon on a bramble just as she was going to the moonbeams' party. Harebell had helped her find some spider's thread, and together they had mended the ribbon.

Then she was going to fly straight to Thorntree Drive, where Suzy lived. Instead she had gone with Snowdrop to the party, and when the moonbeams begged her to stay she had forgotten all about the tooth and the **quarter** and Suzy.

Harebell wept. How could she have been

so selfish? Poor, poor Suzy! How upset and disappointed she must have been when she awoke and found her tooth still there under the pillow.

"I shall give you one more chance," said the Fairy Queen. "Tonight you must go to Suzy's home. I'm sure she will put the tooth under her pillow again. But if you forget this time, I shall never again trust you with an important job."

Harebell could hardly wait for the night to come. At last it did. But what a night! The wind blew hard and the trees swayed up and down and made a dreadful noise. Harebell's little wings soon grew tired and she flew down to rest beside a hedge.

Suddenly she heard a loud squeak, and then another and another. Someone was in trouble.

"What is it?" she called. "Where are you? Can I help?"

There, quite close to Harebell, was a little grey mouse. His whiskers twitched anxiously.

"A branch has fallen on my tail," he told Harebell. "I can't move it. And it does hurt!"

Harebell tried to lift the branch. Luckily, it was only a small one and she managed to raise it just long enough for the mouse to whisk his tail out of the way.

"Is it very sore?" asked Harebell.

"It is rather," said the mouse. "I'd better go back to my hole and bathe it. I wonder — would you come with me? It's difficult putting a bandage on one's own tail."

Harebell touched the little quarter in her pocket. She was about to refuse. Then she looked at the mouse's sad little face and felt so sorry for him that she said, "Of course I'll come with you."

She bandaged the hurt tail, then told the mouse that she must be on her way but she promised to visit him the next day.

Suzy was sleeping peacefully as Harebell gently drew out the little tooth from under the pillow. She put her hand into her pocket to take out the quarter.

It wasn't there! There was nothing there! It must have fallen out of her pocket on the way. But where?

Quickly Harebell popped the tooth back under the pillow and flew back through the windy night to the hole where the mouse lived.

He was squatting at the door, his whiskers twitching and his little black eyes worried. In his front paws he held something carefully...the quarter!

"I found it after you'd gone," he explained happily. "I guessed it was important, but I didn't know where you'd gone, so I couldn't bring it to you."

Harebell was so relieved that she kissed both his little whiskery cheeks.

But it was growing light!

It was nearly morning!

Harebell flew faster than she had ever flown before. What if Suzy should wake early?

But when she reached the bedroom, Suzy still slept peacefully.

Harebell took the tooth from under the pillow again. Then, carefully, she put the shiny quarter in its place. She looked at the sleeping little girl. Then suddenly, she took off the little blue necklace she wore around her neck and popped it under the pillow with the quarter.

"I'm so sorry I forgot," she whispered. "I won't ever do it again."

Sammy's Surprise

by M. Issitt

It was a hot sunny morning and all the animals in the jungle were having a nap before lunch. All the animals, that is, except Sammy the Snake. Sammy was too excited to sleep. You see, this was his birthday, and he was going to ask all his animal friends to tea.

After lunch Sammy slid down from the branch where he had been resting, and set off through the jungle. He decided to call on his friend Olly Elephant first.

"Hello, Sammy, lovely day, isn't it?" said Olly.

"Yes, lovely day," said Sammy. "It's my birthday today, you know. Would you care to come to tea?"

"Your birthday, eh! Well — er — I'm not too sure, I will let you know."

"Goodbye," said Sammy, rather hurt that Olly didn't seem keen to come. Sammy hurried on. He still had lots of friends to call on before tea.

"Hello, Sammy, you're a long way from home today," said Gerry Giraffe as he helped himself to another juicy green leaf high in the tree. "Please excuse me, but I'm having a late lunch. You see, I've had a rather busy morning."

"Carry on," said Sammy, "I just came to ask you to my birthday tea."

"Yes, well, — er — it's most kind of you. I'll let you know later, shall I?"

"Very nice, I'm sure," sighed Sammy.

Sammy made his way to the river bank, where he spied Aggie Alligator rolling about in the water.

"Hello, Sammy, nice weather for the time of year," said Aggie, making her way slowly up the river bank.

"Yes, the weather is lovely," said Sammy. "I've come to ask you to my birthday tea this afternoon."

"Thank you," said Aggie, "that's most kind but I'm not sure if I can make it. I'll let you know, shall I?"

Sammy felt rather lonely as he made his way back through the trees. "I don't understand it at all," he muttered to himself, "as they all came to my tea last year, and they enjoyed it."

Sammy saw Mickey Monkey and his brothers and sisters playing in the trees above him. Mickey Monkey was talking to a huge gathering of birds. Sammy made his way to the top of the tree.

"Good afternoon, everyone," he said, trying to sound more cheerful than he felt. The monkeys and the birds stopped talking and glared at him.

"Er, hello, Sammy, long way from home, aren't you."

"I suppose so," said Sammy. "I came specially to ask you to my birthday tea."

"Oh dear, oh dear, so you're having a birthday tea, are you?" asked Mickey. "I'm not too sure if we can all come, but we will let you know later."

Poor Sammy felt very sad. "No one wants to come to my birthday tea. I don't understand it." He lay down under a huge tree.

"I say, old chap, you look a bit forlorn," said Lenny Lion, "anything wrong?"

"Well, yes," said Sammy, "as a matter of

16

fact no one wants to come to my birthday tea."

"Most sad," said Lenny. "Well, I must be off. I'm rather busy."

"I don't suppose *you* would come to my birthday tea?" asked Sammy hopefully.

"I'm sorry, old chap, rather tied up, you know."

"Goodbye," said Sammy.

It was a very sad little snake that went home. Lovely birthday this had turned out to be indeed! Sammy decided to take a stroll before having an early night.

Sammy made his way through the branches, then suddenly he stopped. "Um, very strange," he whispered, "I can't hear the birds singing or the monkeys chattering. It's very strange."

Sammy set off home and when he arrived he got a lovely surprise.

"Happy birthday to Sammy," sang the birds.

Everyone had come. There was Olly Elephant, Gerry Giraffe, Aggie Alligator, Lenny Lion, Mickey Monkey, his brothers and sisters, and all the birds.

Sammy had lots of presents to open and Lenny Lion had made a beautiful cake with lots of candles on it.

"Oh, how lovely," said Sammy happily, "you all came after all."

"Yes," said Aggie Alligator, "we were trying to plan a surprise birthday tea, but you kept popping up inviting everyone to your tea."

"Oh," said Sammy, "I am a silly snake. I thought you didn't want to come."

Sammy had a lovely birthday after all. The birds sang *For he's a jolly good fellow* and the monkeys did a hornpipe, and everyone enjoyed the party . . . especially Sammy Snake.

THE WIZARD'S KEY

by Sheena Ronsey

Dimblego the wizard went to his spell cupboard and pulled the door. It was locked, and quite right too. A wizard should never forget to lock his spells up safely when he went out. Dimblego rattled the door. The trouble was that he could never remember where he had put the key.

The wizard turned out his pockets. He found a bar of chocolate and the penknife he had lost last week. He hunted all over the room and found a letter he had forgotten to post. So he went out and posted the letter.

"I was looking for something," said Dimblego to himself when he came back, "but what?" He went to his spell cupboard and pulled the door. "Oh yes," he said. "That key."

He looked in the lounge. He swept the hall and looked under the doormat. He opened all the drawers in the kitchen, but he could not find the key. He looked in the larder, and that made him feel hungry. So he had lunch and then went upstairs to clean his teeth. There was the key, hidden in his toothmug. Dimblego was so pleased.

The wizard worked hard all afternoon. When the clock struck six he put everything away and locked the spell cupboard. Then he had an idea. Quickly he unlocked the cupboard and took out a big red book. He turned over the pages and wrote something on his notepad.

"Easy," said Dimblego. "Why didn't I think of it before? A drop of that bottle, a pinch of powder from this box, a few magic words, and — key, key, where are you?"

"In my keyhole," said the key.

The wizard skipped three times round the table. At last he could have a quiet evening by the fire without even trying to remember where he had put that key. He thought his troubles were over, but he had forgotten that sometimes he put the key in his pocket.

Next day the wizard went to his cupboard, and it was locked. He began to look for the key. After a little while he found his notebook, where he had written, "Spell for finding keys." Dimblego laughed. Fancy forgetting that!

"Key, key, where are you?"

"In the coal bucket."

The wizard went into the lounge and emptied the coal bucket. He took out the key and washed it, and put it in his jacket pocket. Then he washed the dishes, which he had forgotten to do after breakfast. He went to the lounge to look for the morning paper and stopped in surprise.

"Dear me," said Dimblego. "How did all that coal dust get on the carpet? I shall have to clean it up."

He fetched a brush and a shovel. He took off his jacket, rolled up his sleeves, and cleaned the carpet. Then he went back to his spell cupboard.

"Key, key, where are you?"

"In your jacket pocket."

Poor Dimblego. He hunted all over the house before he found his jacket. It was no use asking the key, because the key could not see out of the pocket. The wizard found a piece of string in his pocket with the key. So he tied the key on the string and hung it round his neck. After that he always found it quickly, even when he did forget where it was.

Dora Dolphin

by Grace Ford

Dora Dolphin was terribly excited. This was the day she was to have her first film test, and she was busy cleaning her teeth very specially so that her smile would be extra nice. It was taking quite a long time, for she had nearly a hundred of them. "Remember, a nice big smile for the camera, Dora," her mother was saying.

Some other dolphin girls in the Boarding School were also in the Beauty Competition, but most people thought Dora would win. AND THEY WERE RIGHT, she did win!

"And not only is she the prettiest dolphin," said the smiling Lord Mayor announcing her name, "but also she is the best-natured too, and we all wish her the greatest success in her future film career."

Her family were so proud of her as they all came to see her off on her travels: her brothers and sisters — Effie, Jackie, Mandy, Lizzie and Little Davie. Only her mother

wiped away a few dolphin tears with her fin and said, "Remember now, Dora, we'll always be here waiting near the shore, if ever you want to come back to our lovely deep blue sea."

Ah yes, the lovely sea. Dora watched it till she was out of sight.

How happy she'd been there, leaping and jumping up at the white foamy waves, making friends with the seagulls and the men in boats. But now she must forget all that and learn how to become the cleverest Dolphin, perhaps in the whole world!

So Dora had to go back to the Dolphin School again and learn all sorts of new tricks and lessons: jumping through double hoops high up in the air, and playing games with the other pretty dolphins.

"She's marvellous," the trainers and the film directors said. "The best we've ever had. What a sensation she'll be."

They were very careful with her. The great tank was always specially warmed, and every day they watched that she was fit and well. She was treated like a princess, a Dolphin Princess, of course.

Lots of people came to watch her. The children came with their mothers and fathers in special trains, and they clapped their hands and shouted as she went through her tricks. Everyone loved her.

But one day Dora began to feel just a little bit out of sorts, just a little bit tired of always seeing so many people. It wasn't so much fun just doing the same thing every day somehow.

She began to think of her mother, and brothers and sisters. What fun they'd had together, leaping and playing all day long.

The nice trainer began to worry when he saw that she wasn't happy.

"Just a bit off colour," the film directors

said. "She'll soon be all right." But the trainer wasn't satisfied with that and fetched the Dolphin Doctor.

The Doctor was a very nice, kind man and he examined Dora carefully. After a little while, he looked very solemn and said, "If Dora is to be better soon she must go back to the deep blue sea where she came from. She is fretting for her home. She must go back to her brothers and sisters."

Everyone was sad when they heard this, they all loved her so much, especially the nice trainer. But he took her away, back to her own home-shores where she would learn to be happy again.

Her family were all out in the deep blue sea and came in towards the shore swimming strongly and quickly when they saw her. All of them, her mother and brothers and sisters — Effie, Jackie, Mandy, Lizzie and Little Davie (although Little Davie was not nearly so little as he used to be).

"I thought you would come back one day, my dear," said her wise mother. "It was the deep blue sea that made you so pretty and happy. Look," she cried waving a fin to the trainer who was watching them from the beach, "Dora looks better already. You mustn't take her away again."

Soon Dora was leaping and frisking happily about, in and out of the water, just as she used to do. And now she had a lot more tricks to show them.

Lots of people would gather on the shore to watch her, clapping hands and smiling to each other.

Sometimes her trainer would come and watch too. Or he would swim out to her and bring presents of fish, especially herring, which she liked best. He wasn't sad any more that she had left him and the dolphin tank, and he never forgot her.

For he knew that the deep blue sea was her real home.

The TAILOR'S GIFT

Barnaby was the best tailor in the land. He worked so fast that you could hardly see his hands moving as he sewed his straight, strong stitches.

Barnaby made some clothes for the king and his family, but mostly he sewed for ordinary people. And he even sewed for those who could not afford to pay him. Everyone loved kind Barnaby.

When the king's royal tailor died, he asked Barnaby to take his place, and to live in fine rooms in his palace. It was a great honour, and Barnaby agreed to go.

The people were sorry to see Barnaby leave, and they presented him with a gift. The mayor handed Barnaby a tiny pair of scissors and a shiny needle. "It is not a large gift," he said, "but I think you will find it useful."

The next day Barnaby was sitting in the king's palace, sewing an embroidered jacket, when suddenly the new shiny needle jumped from his fingers.

Barnaby watched in amazement as the needle sewed on its own, making stitches that were even straighter and stronger than Barnaby's. When the jacket was finished the scissors snipped the thread.

From that day Barnaby told the needle and scissors what to make, and simply sat on his cushion and watched. The king was delighted with his new clothes, and

Barnaby was able to help some of the poor people who lived near the palace by sewing warm coats for them.

But Barnaby grew lazy. He no longer sewed warm winter coats for the poor people, but slept late every day and spent his time leaning on his bench, snoozing and daydreaming. He didn't notice when the needle grew rusty and sewed big, untidy stitches, and the scissors grew blunt and spoiled the fine cloth . . .

Barnaby didn't notice, but the king *did*. "Barnaby!" he shouted. "I will not be seen in a coat like this! Look at it! It is falling apart!" And the king pulled off a sleeve to prove it.

"I will give you one more chance," the king said. "Princess Louisa is to be married in one week, and I want to wear a splendid new suit for the ceremony. Sew a fine suit for me, or you will be banished from my kingdom."

Barnaby went back to his rooms and told the needle and scissors what to make, but they lay on the bench, rusty and useless. Barnaby sighed. "I'll just have to make it myself," he said, "though I'll be lucky to finish it in a week."

Barnaby worked night and day on the king's suit, his fingers stitching faster than ever. When the night before the wedding arrived he had only a jewelled collar and two cuffs to finish.

As he bent his head over his work, there came a knock on the door. Barnaby opened it and found a very old, bent woman standing outside, shivering in thin rags. "I am so cold, and I need a warm coat," she said. "The mayor told me that you were kind, and would sew one for me."

Barnaby felt so sorry for the old woman that he could not turn her away — even though he would not finish the king's new clothes. He sat her by the fire and started to sew a warm coat for her.

He finished it as dawn was breaking, and put it around her thin shoulders.

"Thank you," said the old woman. "I cannot pay you, but I will polish your needle and scissors instead." She touched the needle and scissors, and they shone like new. Then she disappeared!

Barnaby watched as the needle and scissors set to work on the jewelled collar and cuffs for the king's suit. One hour before the wedding it was finished, and the king was delighted. "But don't grow lazy again," the king warned.

Barnaby took his advice, and from that day he sat stitching clothes for the poor while the shiny needle and scissors sewed the king's clothes. He knew that if he grew lazy again the needle would rust and the scissors grow blunt.

NIGHT AND DAY

by Moira Stubley

Long, long ago, when the world was very young, Night used to fall as suddenly as a clap of thunder. One moment it would be daylight; then, in a flash, nightime began.

But as the years went by, Day and Night grew tired of this. They passed each other every twelve hours, but never exchanged the time of day . . . or night!

"I feel sure I would like the Night," Day murmured to herself. "He seems gentle and protective, with his cover of darkness and the silence he brings to the earth. I wish I could meet him."

"Day is so beautiful," Night would reflect. "If only I could stop to admire her blue skies and brightness."

So, one day, a little before his time, Night sent out his brightest star to twinkle in the sky. Day was enchanted with the star, shining like a splendid jewel in her hair.

"Thank you for your gift," she whispered

in a gentle breeze, as nightime fell.

Early next morning, when the sky was still black with night, Day commanded the Sun to peep over the horizon. Splendid colours of orange and gold spread across the blackness.

"How beautiful we look together," the Night sky whispered, as Day dawned in the heavens.

So it was that the first stars twinkled that Night in the Daylight sky. The Sun and Moon shared the heavens. Shadows lengthened, and glorious colours filled the sky. Little by little, the light faded into dusk. It was the birth of Twilight, the son of Night and Day.

And then, next morning, the colours of Day painted the darkness of the sky. Fading stars twinkled in the rising sunlight. It was the birth of Dawn, the daughter of Day and Night.

So, each beautiful Dawn, you must make a prayer that the coming Day will guide you until Twilight. And, at the gentle Twilight, make another prayer that the Night will protect you until the shining Dawn.

THE DRAGON WHO CAUGHT A COLD

by Mary Graves

It all began when the dragon sneezed. Something like a loud explosion shook the town of Puckleberry, rattling windows and slamming doors. Another sneeze followed just as the Mayor of Puckleberry was coming out of the Town Hall after a meeting. His hat was blown off his head, down the street and into the duck-pond!

"Bless my soul!" exclaimed the Mayor. "They didn't mention gale force winds in the weather forecast."

The people of Puckleberry had grown quite used to the dragon who lived in a cave on top of the hill. True, there had been one or two awkward moments. One year, for instance, the dragon's hot breath had singed all the little Christmas trees growing on the hill. The people had to make do with plastic trees that year.

But this cold was a very different matter! All night long the people were kept awake by the dragon's mighty snuffles and grunts and puffs and snorts. With all those germs flying about it wasn't long before nearly every citizen of Puckleberry had a terrible streaming cold.

Meanwhile, up in his cave, poor Fortescue the dragon was feeling very sorry for himself.

"Nobody comes up here to see me anybore," he snuffled to himself. "I feel so poorly and nobody cares." A big tear trickled down his cheek and rolled down the hillside. Another tear followed and then another . . . and soon a small stream was running down the hillside and into the town.

The Mayor came out of the Town Hall, and stepped straight into a large puddle of

28

water! "Bless my soul!" he exclaimed. "I didn't know it was raining," and he put his umbrella up. Then he sneezed. "A . . . aaaa . . . aaaa . . . choo! Something must be done. We can't go on like this. I'll call a meeting of the Town Council."

The councillors were old and wise and they sat around the table stroking their long white beards and muttering and sneezing.

"He'll have to go," mumbled one.

"He'll have to go," they all echoed, forgetting how glad they had been when the kindly dragon had entertained their children by giving them switch-back rides up and down his long scaly tail.

"We must send him away," they said.

But the question was how? You can't wrap up a dragon in a paper parcel and put him in the post.

Just then the door opened and Rosie came in with cups of tea. Rosie lived in the town and came every day to tidy up for the Mayor and make the tea. She had been visiting her aunt and had not yet heard about the dragon's cold.

"Who must you send away?" she asked.

"Rosie," scolded the Mayor, "how many times have I told you that Council business is secret and you must not listen? Oh well, I suppose you may as well know." And he told her all about it.

Rosie felt very sorry for poor Fortescue. "But there's no need to send him away," she said, "I know just what to do." She beckoned the councillors around her and told them of her plan.

"Are you sure it will work?" asked the Mayor anxiously.

"Positive!" Rosie told him, and the councillors all went home to supper.

That evening, just before it got dark, the dragon saw someone coming up the hill towards his cave. As the figure drew nearer he recognised Rosie.

"What do you want?" he asked very rudely. Rosie was pulling a big basket on wheels.

"My, oh my, you do look poorly," she said. "You're all thin and pale, and you've a terrible red nose."

"Go away," grumbled the dragon. "I don't feel like visitors, especially if they are rude about by nose." He shut his eyes. Then he opened one again. "What's in that basket?" he asked.

Rosie told him she had brought some thick blankets and a hot water bottle to keep him warm. She tucked him in cosily.

"You'll soon be better," she assured him. "Just drink this up and it will do you the world of good." She unscrewed a bottle and poured some steaming liquid into a cup.

"What is it?" asked the dragon warily.

"It's a hot posset," Rosie told him.

"What's a posset?" asked Fortescue very suspiciously.

"It's an old-fashioned warm drink. This is my old granny's recipe and it's very good."

"Is it medicine?"

"In a way, I suppose."

"Shan't drink it!" declared the dragon, turning his face to the wall.

"Suit yourself!" said Rosie. "But if you don't get better they will send you away."

Fortescue sat up quickly. "They wouldn't dare — would they?" he quavered.

"Oh yes, they would," answered Rosie.

The dragon was silent, then he looked at the drink. "Does it taste nasty?"

"No," Rosie comforted him. "Here, drink it quickly."

The dragon took a tiny sip, then another, and as soon as the cup was empty he fell fast asleep.

Rosie had warned the Mayor that the dragon would snore, and snore he most certainly did all that night. It was just like a thunderstorm without the lightning.

But early next morning he awoke, feeling brighter than a new pin.

"I feel fine," he shouted to Rosie as soon as he saw her coming up the hill, "I could dance a jig!"

"Please don't," Rosie begged.

"Remember how dangerous your great tail can be when you start swinging it around. Look," she went on, "I've made a lovely thick curtain to hang across your cave doorway. I think you were in a draught when those cold March winds were blowing."

The dragon was ever so grateful.

Rosie would never tell anyone what was in the posset, but whatever it was must have damped the dragon's hot breath because he was never able to breathe out fire and smoke again. The people of Puckleberry were all delighted and were able to grow some beautiful Christmas trees on the hill.

Fortescue never had another cold, but he frequently asked for a hot posset... because he thought he had one coming!

POOR PRINCE PEREGRINE

by Anne Robertson

Once upon a time, in a faraway country, lived a young Prince. He lived in a grand palace with his parents, the King and Queen, who loved him dearly.

They gave him Icicle, a magnificent white horse to ride, and Snowy, a lovable white puppy to play with.

But in spite of all these things, Peregrine was the poorest person in the whole kingdom. He had everything he could desire to make him happy, except the most important gift of all. A heart! In its place was a cold lump of ice!

Peregrine could not love the King and Queen. This made them very sad.

Peregrine could not love Icicle. He left him alone in his stable, and the horse did so want to please him.

Peregrine could not love Snowy. He never patted him or took him for walks in the palace garden.

Peregrine could not love anyone or anything, and this made him very unhappy.

One day, feeling more unhappy than usual, Peregrine walked out of the palace. He took no notice of Snowy, who ran at his heels. He took no notice of Icicle, who stared at him from the open stable door.

Sadly, he walked in the forest. It was very, very cold, but the Prince could not feel it, his heart was so cold already.

It began to snow. Little flakes at first, then bigger ones.

As Peregrine sadly trudged along, his clothes were soon caked with snow. They became so heavy that he had to stop. He tried to brush away the thick snow, but it was frozen hard.

He tried to walk again, but found he could not move his legs. He could not lift his arms either. He was frozen solid. Just like a snowman!

A little field mouse came scurrying along. He stopped beside the snowman.

"Oh dear. I can't find my way home in all this snow!" cried the little field mouse.

Peregrine stared at the little field mouse. He had never felt sorry for anyone or anything in his life before but, suddenly, he was filled with pity.

"That little creature is more unfortunate than I!" he thought with surprise. So he said, "If you can burrow inside the snow, you will be safe here."

"Thank you, snowman!" said the field mouse. He dug away the snow and curled himself up on the Prince's slippers and went to sleep.

Suddenly, inside the thick snow, Peregrine's feet began to tingle.

"Oh!" he thought in astonishment. "My feet feel so strange! They are quite warm!"

Nothing like that had ever happened to him before!

Then, a robin flew down and perched upon the snowman's shoulder. "I'm so hungry!" he cried.

Once again, Peregrine was filled with pity for the unfortunate creature. So he said kindly, "Robin, if you look inside my glove,

"Please take it!" insisted the Prince.

As she took off the Prince's old jacket, a single tear rolled down her cheek onto the snowy breast of the snowman. She wrapped the jacket around her thin body, and said, "Thank you! I am lovely and warm *now*!" And she ran off.

you will find a biscuit I was saving for myself!"

"Thank you, snowman!" said the robin happily, and he hopped down onto Peregrine's hand and pulled back his frozen glove. Then, with the biscuit in his beak, he flew away to the nearest tree to eat it.

The Prince's hand began to tingle. "Now my hand feels strange too! It's warm, just like my feet!" he thought in astonishment.

It was snowing harder than ever when the little girl came into the forest. In her thin frock she stood beside the snowman, and shivered.

"M-my f-father h-has s-ent m-me t-to g-gather w-wood f-for t-the f-fire, b-but I-I'm s-so c-cold!" Cristal's teeth chattered so she could hardly speak.

Once again, Peregrine was moved to pity. So he said kindly, "You shall have my coat to keep you warm!"

Cristal looked at the snowman in surprise. "But you need it yourself!" she said.

Suddenly Peregrine felt very warm. He glowed. The girl's tear had penetrated his body and melted the block of ice that was his heart. Quickly, the thick snow melted and fell away.

Then the Prince did another strange thing — he smiled!

He ran all the way home to the palace.

The King and Queen stared in astonishment at his smiling face.

He rushed up to them, and kissed them. "Oh, I do love you!" he cried.

That made them very happy.

Then Snowy bounded up to him. Peregrine patted the little puppy affectionately on the head. That made Snowy very happy.

Then, Peregrine ran to the stable. He fondled Icicle and stroked his soft nose. That made the horse very happy.

Then Peregrine hurried back to the King and Queen. He walked out onto the balcony with them.

When the people saw their happy King and Queen, standing with their smiling, happy Prince, they cried, "Look! Peregrine has a heart! It is warm and kind!"

They were happy too!

SALLY SWALLOW'S PROBLEM

by Grace Ford

"There she goes again," cried Sally's mother with a sigh. "I told her to turn left at the corner tree and she's gone right. She'll never, never learn."

Ever since Sally was a tiny bird learning to fly, she had always got mixed up with her lefts and rights. She just laughed it off, saying, "There's always someone to put me right."

"That's all very well," her mother would say. "But what about when we start off on the Great Journey south?"

"Well, *what* about it?"

Her mother looked anxious.

"That's when all the swallows leave their homes and fly thousands of miles south to the lovely countries where skies are so blue, and the sun shines warm for ever. We couldn't stay here for winter. It is so very cold."

Sally thought the change would be very nice.

"But what's my left and right got to do with the blue sky and the sunshine?"

"Everything," explained her mother. "You see, we all get together on the trees and bushes and telegraph wires and then divide into groups. There is a leader for each group and we must all do what he says. He tells us when to start and when and where to rest. If he signals LEFT and you go RIGHT, you will lose us. We can't stop and you would never find your way alone. It's a long, long journey, and we get very tired."

"Oh I'll manage somehow," cried Sally gaily, hopping on one claw.

All her mother said was, "I'm afraid you won't."

Mr. Martinet was passing by, holding himself very erect and looking everywhere at the same time.

"Training this youngster of yours in the way she should go?" he said, looking down his beak at the trembling Sally. "Come, let me see you drilling. *Left, right: Left, right.*"

She got such a fright that not only did she mix up her lefts and rights more than ever, but she seemed to have an extra claw that she didn't know about.

"This will never do!" cried Mr. Martinet. "At this rate you'll be the first to fall, and spoil the whole formation." He was very angry.

Her mother was very worried. The following day she happened to see two little girls playing with their dolls under a tree. One said, "Why have you got wool tied round your finger?" The other explained she was always forgetting things, and this was to remind her to wash her dolly's hair that night.

What a good idea, thought Sally's mother. The very thing to remind the little swallow. She found some sheep's wool caught on a fence, and wound it round and round Sally's right claw.

"Now, remember, Sally, I'm tying this round your RIGHT claw. Keep thinking of it all the time. The one with the wool is RIGHT."

So Sally kept repeating it, and repeating it. This makes it much easier, she thought, for of course the *other* one must be Left.

When the great day came, there was already a sharpness in the air. It seemed as if all the swallows in the world perched in fields, trees and hedges. She was still saying, "Wool is RIGHT, wool is RIGHT." When it was the turn of their section to rise in flight, Mr. Martinet cried, "Vee formation, please, young ones to the front, and to the RIGHT." Sally had no hesitation at all while her mother watched proudly.

People below stopped to look up and watch the swallows out of sight. "How wonderful — not one out of step. Formation perfect, but it means Summer is ending."

But for Sally it was just beginning.

AN APPLE

by G. Ford

Peter heard the *clippity clop* of the milk horse, and ran down the garden path. "Wait, wait, Dobbin," he shouted, "I've got something for you!"

The red-faced man who brought the milk every day stopped at the gate. "Would Dobbin like this apple Mummy has given me?" Peter asked. "I'm afraid it's not quite fresh."

The man laughed and said, "Just you watch this." And he took the apple and held it out to the horse.

Dobbin took one great bite. Then he munched and munched, showing his big yellow teeth as if he were smiling. He rolled his tongue over his lips again and again. *Did he like apples*! He was mad about them, even giving Peter a little push with his nose

as if to say, "I'd like another one, please — anytime."

Peter laughed with pleasure. "Maybe next time," he promised.

But Mummy only said, "I'll remember when there's any left over. I'll keep one for Dobbin."

He wished now he hadn't spent his pocket money on that silly toy motor. But at least he could go and look at the fruit shop window, and choose something nice just in case he should be rich suddenly one day when he wasn't expecting it.

He turned the corner. But a tall man was running for a bus and knocked against some vegetable boxes on the wooden ledge outside the fruit shop. He didn't stop to pick up the fruit and potatoes that were rolling

FOR DOBBIN

"There's never any danger of *your* milk not being delivered," remarked the milkman one day. "Dobbin thinks your house is much more important than even the Lord Mayor's!"

And so it was, to Dobbin anyhow, far more important. Don't you think so, too?

about on the pavement.

Peter ran to help. "Where shall I put them?" he asked Mrs Brown. She was a very nice person, and often chatted to him when his Mummy bought things.

"Just lay them down beside the left-over fruit in the back shop," she said.

His eyes widened when he saw the heap of rather withered apples in a corner. "If — if you please, Mrs Brown, what are you going to do with those apples?" he asked shyly.

"Well," she answered, "they're not quite fresh. I'll try to sell the best of them, but I daresay I'll have to throw some away. Why do you ask, I wonder?"

Peter hopped about in excitement. "Oh, Mrs Brown, I know the loveliest horse and he's mad about apples, even the old ones. Do you think you could . . .?"

"Of course I could," she cried heartily. "You just help yourself, lad. You helped me so now it's my turn."

Next morning when the milk horse came, Peter was waiting at the gate. He laughed again to see Dobbin munch and munch. "More tomorrow," promised Peter.

Soon the friendly brown horse started neighing at the gate till Peter came out, whether he had apples or not. He loved getting his soft velvety nose stroked by the boy.

THE KINDLY GIRAFFE

by Margery Robinson

George the Giraffe walked sadly round the park where he lived with all the other animals. He had loved living there until Polly the Parrot had come to live there too.

Polly, swinging on her perch, made remarks about everybody. But as all the animals took no notice of her silly words, Polly soon stopped . . . except whenever she saw the Giraffe.

"Washed your neck today?" or "Is it cold up there?" she would call, which she followed by a screeching laugh. This made George so unhappy that he longed to hide his lovely long neck.

"Take no notice," said the heron, peacefully paddling among the weeds. "She shouldn't be so rude, but I don't think she means it. Anyway, long necks and long legs too can be very useful," and off she went to the other end of the lake.

George tried not to notice Polly, but he was still unhappy.

The next morning, George went for his usual walk very early. Even Polly was asleep. He was glad that he had missed her raucous shriek.

At the farther end of the park he found the small gate, used only by the keepers, standing open. Someone had forgotten to close it. This was his chance to get away from Polly.

Carefully he pushed the gate wide open, taking care to close it behind him with his nose before he set off on the grass verge.

Happily he sniffed the air. It was going to be a lovely day, he told himself, as he walked along with big strides.

Soon he came to a village. Everything looked clean and bright. There was a lady up a ladder cleaning her windows. As George passed she dropped one of her dusters.

George bent his long neck, picked it up in his mouth and handed it back to her.

"Oh, thank you. How kind you are, it has saved me climbing down." She looked at George and patted his neck gently. "Such a lovely long neck. Are you coming to our fête? I hope that you will have fun today." And she began to polish her windows again.

George wondered what a fête was. It must have something to do with all the flags which were fluttering in the breeze.

Near the village green George heard a little girl sobbing. She was standing under a tree with a small boy. "How can we get Tibbles down? Mummy says we will have to leave him there until after the fête."

George looked into the tree. High on one of the branches was a tiny kitten clinging to the top of the tree. He was so scared that he 'miaowed' every time the wind swayed the branches. He will fall down if he isn't rescued, thought George.

Now George knew all about kittens with scratchy claws, so he went behind and gently caught the kitten by the scruff of his neck. Very carefully he lowered Tibbles until he was near the ground. The little girl caught him safely as he landed.

"Thank you, dear Giraffe." She put her arms round George's neck as he bent down. Gently she kissed him. "If it hadn't been for you, Tibbles would have had to stay up there all day."

George strolled along, looking at all the sideshows, until he came to the church, where everybody was standing looking up at the clock.

"It's stopped," said a policeman, "now we'll never know when to begin the fête. I must tell the Mayor."

"It's just been cleaned especially for the fête," said an old lady. "Where's Mr. Biggs with his long ladder? He'll soon start it again."

"Oh dear!" said the Mayor crossly, coming out of the church. "Biggs, Biggs, where's Biggs?" But no Mr. Biggs appeared. He had gone to another village to mend their clock and wouldn't be back until the afternoon.

"Too late!" growled the Mayor twiddling his chain round and round. "Whatever shall we do? It only wants a nudge to get it going."

The Giraffe had been standing quietly listening. He knew that if he stretched his neck he could reach the hands . . . but could he move the hands with his nose?

While everyone was arguing, George started to push the long hand round. It turned easily, then it chimed the hour.

They all looked startled, then began to smile as the clock ticked on.

The Mayor looked at his large watch. "The clock's exactly right. Such a useful long neck, Giraffe. You deserve a reward."

"He lifted my kitten down from the tree," said the small girl, who had joined the crowd.

"And picked up my duster," said a lady.

"A kind Giraffe, too. I must find him something special. Wait until I go to the

42

Town Hall." Getting into his car the Mayor disappeared down the lane.

"Home, George, my lad," said a voice behind the Giraffe, who was enjoying himself so much. "Why did you run away? I've been looking everywhere for you. What have you been doing? It's long past your breakfast time." The keeper wiped his hot face.

Everyone started to tell the keeper all that had been happening. The keeper was very proud of George. He had a cup of tea while waiting for the Mayor to come back.

"Bend your head down," said the Mayor, slipping a scarlet ribbon on to George's neck as everybody clapped.

George looked down. On the ribbon was a bright medal. He strutted round, showing it to everybody.

"It's nearly dinnertime and you've had no breakfast," said the keeper, leading George back towards the park.

Inside the park there was a commotion. Polly was screeching, "Get me down. Get me down." Her feathers were tangled in the string of a large kite which had lodged in the trees.

Her keeper had gone to fetch a long ladder, but Polly was so scared.

For a moment George hesitated, then he stretched his long neck up and gently caught hold of Polly's legs. Carefully he brought her down, with the kite flapping behind her.

Polly said nothing until her feathers were unwound and she was back on her perch.

"Thank you very much, Giraffe, for rescuing me," she said quietly.

"I hope," said the heron severely, "that you will always remember that a long neck is better than a raucous shriek any day."

Bear in a Bush

by Julie Horton

Theobold Rabbit hopped happily through the wood.

"Hello, deer!" he called to a family of deer. "I'm going to tea with Angela Hare and I shall have sticky buns and play with her sweet little babies."

"Have a good time," called the deer in their gentle voices.

He hopped on and nearly landed on Frank Frog.

"*Whoops*! Sorry, Frank," he called. "I can't stop. I'm going to tea with Angela Hare and I shall have sticky buns and play with her sweet little babies."

"Have a good time," croaked Frank Frog.

Theobold hopped on. He was in the very dark part of the wood now and it was a bit creepy.

Suddenly he stopped.

"I don't like the look of that bush in front!" he thought.

Something rustled inside the bush.

"And I certainly don't like the sound of

it!" he squeaked. "There's something there and it could be a bear!"

He heard footsteps behind him.

"Oh, help!" he squeaked.

But it was only Sid Squirrel.

"Hello, Theo!" said Sid. "Why are you staring at that bush?"

"Hello, Sid!" said Theo. "I'm staring at this bush because there is a bear in it, and I am afraid to pass. But if I don't pass, I won't

"Hello, Theo and Sid," she said. "Why are you staring at that bush?"

"Hello, Lara," said Sid. "We are staring at this bush because there is a lion in it and we are afraid to pass. And poor Theo will not be able to have tea with Angela Hare, and he won't have any sticky buns, and he won't be able to play with the dear little babies."

"What a shame!" cried Lara. "Let me listen."

And she listened to the rustling in the bush. And her eyes grew bigger and bigger.

"That's not a lion," she whispered. "That's a gorilla! And I am afraid to pass too."

have tea with Angela Hare, and I won't have sticky buns, and I won't be able to play with her sweet little babies."

"What a shame!" said Sid. "Let me listen."

And he listened to the rustling in the bush. And his eyes grew rounder and rounder.

"That's not a bear," he whispered. "That's a lion! And I'm scared stiff!"

"Hello!" called a voice behind them.

"Oh, help!" squeaked Theo and Sid.

But it was only Lara the Fox Cub.

"Hello!" called a voice behind them.

"Oh, help!" squeaked Theo and Sid and Lara. But it was only old Shamus the Badger.

"Oh, Mr Badger," cried Lara, "we are so glad to see you. There is a gorilla in that bush and none of us dare pass it."

"Nonsense!" grinned Shamus. "Let me have a look."

And he marched right up to the bush and stuck his head inside . . . and out flew a very cross thrush.

"Really!" she twittered. "I can't even build a nest without badgers barging in." And she flew away across the wood.

"There's your gorilla!" chuckled Shamus, as he shuffled off down the path.

Feeling very small and very silly, Theo, Sid and Lara crept past the bush and down the path to Angela's house.

Angela was very pleased to see them. She said there were enough sticky buns for all of them, and asked them very nicely if they would play with her babies, so that she could have a rest and a sticky bun herself.

LOOPY GOES FLYING

by Roger James

Loopy longed to fly. Ever since his early childhood he had watched enviously as the birds soared and glided above him. His friends thought him foolish. After all, whoever heard of a caterpillar who could fly?

At first the other caterpillars had watched Loopy's flying attempts with some interest. He would rush across the cabbage leaf and hurl himself into the air — only to land with a sickening thud on the earth below. Soon he became quite an attraction. Tickets would be sold for front row seats and caterpillars would crawl for miles for a good view of Loopy's antics. Loopy could never

really understand why others found his flying attempts so funny — after all, this was his life's ambition and he took it all very seriously.

As he grew older and bigger he climbed higher and became more daring. He also thought a little more about the business of flying and how the birds managed to do it so easily. "For a start," he observed from his leaf at the top of the raspberry cane, "they have wings and that must be quite a help."

Some days later, whilst nibbling through a tasty leaf he came upon a toffee paper carelessly left there by the wind. "Ideal!" he thought and within an hour, by carefully

47

sewing the paper to some small twigs with his own silk, he had fashioned a fine set of wings.

Friends helped to pull the wings to the edge of the leaf and, as Loopy climbed aboard, the crowd fell silent. With a heave he was off and gliding to the ground. The crowd cheered wildly but then the home-made aeroplane began to spin. It turned like a top, then flipped upside down. Loopy hung on for his life. Still spinning, it crashed into the ground a few yards away. A very dizzy Loopy crawled from under the wing and tottered away with the howls of laughter from the crowd still ringing in his ears.

Slowly he began the long hard climb back to the top of the raspberry cane, hauling the broken wings behind him.

"I must be too heavy," he decided. "I shall have to make bigger wings."

Within a week the new wings were ready. They were fine wings; sleek, shiny and pale brown in colour.

This time only a few turned up to watch the flight. Most caterpillars had seen enough of Loopy's failures — but those who didn't bother to come missed Loopy's greatest achievement.

The wings were a complete failure, of course, and crashed straight to the ground,

but when Loopy was flung from the spinning wings, he glided to safety — and to thunderous applause — on a spider's web parachute.

It was a contented Loopy who crawled exhausted back to the top of the raspberry cane. The bigger wings hadn't worked too well but at least no one had laughed. He was so tired that he felt he must sleep.

"Next flight," he thought, "I will spin silk to fix myself to the wing so that I won't spin off. In fact, I'd better do it now before I fall asleep." He yawned. "I feel as if I could sleep forever."

He began to spin his silk and soon the job was finished. He had made a neat little cockpit for his aeroplane and soon he was snuggled up inside and fast asleep.

He slept for a long time and woke up feeling much better and rather different for his long sleep.

"Time to get flying again," he thought and began to nibble his way out of the cocoon he had made for himself. Getting out was not easy because he seemed to have grown while he was asleep, but finally he squeezed out of the tiny hole and rested for a while on the leaf.

He stretched his aching limbs and wriggled his wings and . . . "WINGS!" he cried, "I wriggled my wings! But I don't have any wings!"

Then he looked behind him. He did have wings, beautiful, sleek, brown wings. He was no longer a caterpillar; he was a beautiful moth.

Overjoyed, he leapt into the air and flew. He soared and dived and soared again. Words could not describe his happiness. Now he *knew* why he had always wanted to fly.

Gypsy Cuckoo comes to Tippett's Wood

by Jean Mathews

One day Suki, the dainty red squirrel, was busy scraping some carrots for dinner.

Suddenly, a *tip-tap, tip-tap* made her stop and listen.

"Why, there's someone at the front door. I wonder who that can be," thought Suki as she ran to open it. But the doorstep was empty. "That's funny, I'm sure I heard a knock. It must have been the wind."

She didn't see Gypsy Cuckoo disappear round the back of Nut Cottage. Gypsy Cuckoo had just arrived in Tippett's Wood and had spent all morning looking for a home. But, do you know, there wasn't one empty house in the whole of Tippett's Wood. So she had an idea.

"If I can't find an empty house, I'll steal a home from someone else." So, when she spotted Blackbird House, her green eyes glinted, "Why, that's just the place!" she exclaimed. "It looks so cosy!"

And it certainly did, snuggling in the branches of the old oak tree, high above Nut Cottage. But it belonged to Mr and Mrs Black.

"Oh dear," thought Gypsy, "I wish they would hurry up and go shopping. I want to move in right now!"

She was getting very impatient and tip-tapped with her beak against the old oak tree. What a shock she got when Suki opened the front door. She hadn't noticed a door there!

Then Gypsy spotted Mr. and Mrs. Black leaving their little house.

"Ah, now's my chance!" And Gypsy Cuckoo sprinted up the steps to Blackbird House. She flung the door wide open and marched in. There inside were Mr. and Mrs. Black's three children.

"Out you go!" ordered Gypsy Cuckoo. "Go and find your Mummy and Daddy."

My goodness, they were frightened ...
Gypsy looked so fierce! They stumbled
down the steps and stood huddled together
outside Nut Cottage.

Suki leaned out of her kitchen window.

"Whatever's the matter?" she wanted to
know.

The children told their sad tale and Suki
was angry. She hurried to Blackbird House
to see Gypsy Cuckoo.

But Gypsy tossed her head and her big
brass earrings jingled as she said, "I'm not
moving from this house. I'm tired and I'm
going to bed." She slammed the door in
Suki's face, and Suki went back home.

Willy the hare was playing with the
children and he said, "Let's try some magic
to frighten her out of the house."

Now Willy's magic isn't very good.
Sometimes it works—but often it doesn't.
Suki crossed her fingers, hoping for the
best. Willy twitched his nose ... once ...
twice ... and then they heard it ... the faint
cries of Gypsy Cuckoo calling "Help, help,
somebody get me down from here!"

Suki and the children gazed up in

amazement at Blackbird House, while Willy danced with delight. His magic had worked and the house was rocking from side to side!

"Help, somebody help me," yelled Gypsy again. "I feel sick!"

Suki giggled as she called out, "All right . . . wait a minute!"

Willy twitched his nose three times to stop the magic—but, oh dear, this time something went wrong. The house did stop rocking, but it started jumping up and down instead! Willy was very puzzled.

"That shouldn't have happened," he confessed to Suki. "Now what do I do?"

"Leave it to me," said a cheery voice behind them. It was Nibs. Now Nibs was a rabbit with a *very* magic nose. He twitched his magic nose and, hey presto, Blackbird House stopped moving about.

Gypsy Cuckoo staggered out of the house and down the steps. Her tawny feathers were ruffled, and her green head-scarf had fallen down over one eye. She had even lost an earring! What a sight she looked! Everyone felt sorry for her. So while

Suki took Mr. and Mrs. Black's three children home again, Willy and Nibs invited Gypsy into Nut Cottage for a cup of tea.

"Why don't you build your own house," asked Nibs and Willy, when Gypsy had finished her tea.

"What . . . me? Don't be silly. I wouldn't know how."

"Well, if you like we'll help," offered Willy, "if you promise one thing . . . "no more house-stealing."

"Oh, I'll never do *that* again," promised Gypsy.

And she never did. But, as you all know, other cuckoos do.

THE LITTLE WOODEN CLOTHES PEG

by Grace Ford

The little clothes peg lay quietly in the peg-basket, feeling lonely and sad although there were lots of other pegs beside her. But they were all made of plastic, all brightly coloured: blue, yellow and red.

She was the only one made of dark thick wood. "If only they'd speak to me," Peggie Clothespeg sighed. "But they all look too smart to bother with me."

When the next washing-day came, she was clipped on to a dazzling white sheet over the clothes rope in the garden, along with the others. She was happy to be so high up and away from the others at last, swinging to and fro in the breeze, above the flowers.

But presently the breeze grew into a wind. And the wind was so strong that she was shot through the air to land with a plop on the grassy drying green below.

"I do hope they'll pick me up soon," she thought. "I don't want to be trodden on and perhaps broken."

Who should pick her up but the little brown and white puppy belonging to the man of the house! Round and round the green he raced, throwing her up in the air and catching her in his sharp little teeth. She didn't like that at all!

But soon the puppy tired and ran upstairs in the house to his master's room with Peggie still in his mouth!

The man was busy at a big desk covered with books and papers and didn't look up. The puppy knew very well that he must be quiet. So he dropped the peg on the carpet, but he was so tired with running about that he soon fell fast asleep at the man's feet.

Suddenly the man pushed the papers aside and stood up to look out of the window.

"Goodness me, where do all my papers get to?" he said crossly. "That's another one gone missing. If only I had a nice big clip to grip them all together —" Then he stopped suddenly and looked on the floor.

There, just in front of him, was the little wooden peg!

"The very thing," he thought. And he knew very well how it got there, for the puppy was always bringing things in from the garden. He bent and patted the puppy. "Clever little dog," he said. "It's just what I wanted."

He soon found the papers he had lost, and clipped them tightly together, placing the bundle in a big leather writing case with handles. He was catching a train for an important meeting, and kept taking the papers out and reading them. Peggie

That is why the little clothes peg sits proudly on top of the man's big desk beside all the books and papers and pens and pencils and the writing machine, that all belong to this famous writer of stories for people and children all over the world.

If ever she gets mislaid or covered by papers, the man gets excited and cross, and shouts "Where is that little clothes peg of mine? I can't write a thing without it. Someone come and help me find it."

Then he looks very hard at the puppy, who is always up to some mischief or other. But the puppy just looks back hard at *him*. For he wouldn't dare run off with that queer piece of wood his master is so fond of, he really wouldn't!

Clothespeg was very excited at travelling so far — no need for the plastic pegs to be so proud, after all this, she thought! Presently she was taken out of the leather case, with all the papers clipped together by herself, and she felt quite important.

An elderly man with white hair had picked them up and when he saw the clothes peg grip, he smiled. "Goodness me," he said, "I haven't seen one of these old wooden pegs since I was a boy. I used to help my mother hang out the clothes on wash day."

When they got back home, the puppy was there waiting to welcome them.

"Good boy," said the man, "for bringing me in the clothes peg. It has brought me luck, for they've accepted all my fairy stories at the bookshop. And from now on, this little clothes peg will be my mascot."

WISE OLD WORLD

by Carole Etherington

Mr World was spinning sadly on his way when one day he said to himself: "The people I carry on my back are rather selfish. It would do them good to live elsewhere. I shall teach them all a lesson."

So he came to a sudden stop. There was a terrific crash as all the people went soaring through the air and came down with a bump in a different country.

"What terrible weather!" exclaimed the English on their first day in Greenland.

"Isn't the snow horrible?" they moaned on the second day.

The weather stayed exactly the same, and by the end of the week they had run out of things to say. So they began to talk to each other and once they had started they could not stop. They soon discovered that they were all really very friendly. They invented a new game of umbrella ice hockey, and they all became very good at scoring goals in black bowler hats.

Meanwhile, the French were in England, and there was chaos in the streets. Some were walking on the right and some were driving on the left. No one knew which way to look first, and everyone was shouting and bumping into everyone else.

The Chinese were in France and they

were starving. They just could not use knives and forks. Each time they got their fork near their mouth the food toppled off. So they raided the knitting shops and carried off all the needles to use as chopsticks.

In Iceland the Arabs were using their

prayer mats as toboggans – when they weren't tripping over their long white robes and falling down fishing holes.

In Switzerland the little Pygmies had made the alpenhorns into stilts. They were coping very well with the tall mountains and the deep valleys.

In the tall jungles of the Amazon the Indians had invented a clever transport system. By hanging up their turbans and their snakes they were able to swing from tree to tree almost as fast as the monkeys.

The stern Russians found themselves on the beautiful tropical island of Fiji. It was so hot that their frosty faces began to thaw. They exchanged their fur hats and coats for short grass skirts. Very soon they were doing hula-hula dances around the island and enjoying themselves so much that they could not stop smiling.

Meanwhile, in Japan, the Norwegians were having a terrible time. They were so big and everything in Japan was so small. They couldn't get in at the doors without bumping their heads, and at night they had to sleep with their feet out of the windows.

So Mr World sent a wind to Japan which picked up all the leaves and feathers and tickled the feet at the windows until their owners cried with laughter.

When Mr World saw that everyone had learnt their lesson he returned them to their own country.

"What fun!" he said. "I feel much happier now that the world is a kinder place."

And, sure enough, it was. The English talked to each other as well as to their foreign friends. The French stopped shouting at them when they went the wrong way round their roundabouts. The Chinese quite understood when their foreign visitors could not use chopsticks, and the Russians beamed and smiled and made everyone welcome. The Norwegians even sent the Japanese a present of extra small skis.

"I shall have to stop more often," said Mr World, spinning happily on his way.

THE NAUGHTY CALF

by G. Ford

Daisy was a gentle cow with pretty brown and white markings. She always kept an eye on the young calves brought into the field for pasture. She would often say, "Don't eat the leaves of that big yew tree over there, whatever you do."

It was a lovely field. When the sun shone on the buttercups and daisies it looked like a big coloured carpet with soft green edges. A little stream ran alongside.

And it tasted so sweet, that meadow! The cows and calves munched away happily day after day the whole summer.

Next to the field was an old church with a great yew tree by the wall. Its branches reached right down, and often made dark shadows over part of the field.

It was lovely to lie in the cool shade when the sun was hot, as long as they remembered that Daisy said they were not to eat those leaves or they would be sick.

But this summer there was one little calf who was always grumbling. Rosie was the pretty one and like to be petted and fussed over.

"I don't like the grass this side of the field," she would say. Or else it would be, "These hedges have holes in them and the wind comes roaring in."

One day she kept bothering Daisy, saying, "Why mustn't we eat the leaves of that horrid old yew tree? If it's not good for us why is it there?"

"No good!" cried Daisy angrily. "The day

will come when you'll be very glad of it. That yew tree is a very old friend of mine. It's been there for hundreds of years, and it makes a lovely shelter." She was quite cross with the naughty calf.

Rosie sulked all that morning. The sun was very hot and she was restless. Presently she said to one of her calf friends, "I'm not afraid of what old Daisy says about the yew leaves. I'm going to taste them."

Off she went to where the branches hung over into the field and began to nibble a tiny bit of the leaf. It tasted horrid. It was hard and leathery and Rosie quickly spat it out. "Ugh," she cried, "I don't want any more of that."

But her little friend had already run to Daisy to tell her. Rosie felt very silly when they both came running up quite out of breath.

"I — I didn't really swallow it, Daisy. It tasted awful." But she did feel a bit queer and lay down.

Daisy shook her head. "Go down to the stream and drink some of the nice cool water. Then lie under the shady yew tree here. You won't find a nicer spot to lie. Everything in the world has some use, and the yew tree is for giving shade, not for eating."

So the little calf lay down under the dark cool shadow. Presently the summer sounds of bees humming and water trickling past made her fall asleep. When she awoke she was as right as rain.

Daisy was pleased to see her better. "My yew tree never loses its leaves, even in winter. The snow is never so deep under it as under other trees and we are always glad to have its shelter, whatever the weather."

After her fright Rosie thought she would always pay attention to what Daisy said. It wasn't much fun sulking half the day, much better to skip about with the other calves and nibble the fresh grass and flowers.

Clovis Kitten's First Christmas

by Carole Etherington

Clovis Kitten was curled up in a corner of the best armchair. His teeth were chattering together — *yak, yak, yak, yak* — and he was squeaking to himself in delight — *eek, eek, eek* — as he dreamt of the mice he would catch when he was grown up.

Suddenly the door opened and a magnificent tree was carried into the room. Clovis Kitten sat up in fright as the tall tree advanced towards him like a prickly rocket.

Just as it was about to touch the tip of his whiskers it stopped. It turned towards the ceiling and came to rest in a big tub of soil waiting for it on the living-room floor.

Clovis's eyes went wider and wider as boxes and bags were piled up on the chairs. They were full of beautiful tinsel, tiny fairy lights and sparkling glass balls.

Clovis jumped down from his chair and tiptoed towards the tree. He lifted his small, pink nose to the lowest branch and sniffed.

"*Eeoow!*" he cried, springing backwards in fright and shaking the sharp pine needle from his nose.

Then he crept around the back of the tree. Round and round, nearer and nearer he went, his ears sloping, his legs bent, his white tummy close to the ground. Then he pounced. He jumped at the tree, attacking the trunk with his claws, biting at the branches, flicking his tail backwards and forwards, going higher and higher until . . . he fell, twisting and tumbling down into the tub.

As Clovis lay panting on the floor, his mischievous eyes caught sight of a long, glittering strand of red tinsel. It was hanging out of a big bag and it was moving very slightly. Clovis's eyes grew wide. He rolled himself upright and moved silently to the side of the tub. He crouched there watching, his head low, his whole body trembling in excitement.

Then he started to flick his long black tail and he began to wiggle his little black bottom, slowly at first, then faster and faster until ... his strong black feet sprang from the floor as though he had bounced off a giant trampoline.

He sped across the room, a streak of black and white fur. Then he pounced on the tinsel, tugging at it and biting it, rolling on his back and boxing at it with his tiny white-gloved paws. And then ... *crash!* The bag on the chair above him overturned, showering Clovis Kitten with shiny glass balls and twinkling stars.

"What a marvellous game," thought Clovis. Round and round the room he went, patting the balls with one paw then with the other, playing with two or three at once like an expert footballer. He dived under the tree, wrapping himself in tinsel as he went. And then ... *pouff!* He collapsed into a soft bed of red and white tinsel and dropped fast asleep.

When he awoke he found himself back in his chair. There in the opposite corner was the tree. Clovis could hardly believe his eyes; he thought it was the prettiest tree he had ever seen, sparkling with tiny stars and gold and silver balls, its lights twinkling and dancing on the green branches. At the foot of the tree were parcels.

Clovis jumped down from the chair and went to investigate. He poked his nose between the boxes and patted the shiny wrapping paper. Then he began to sniff and sniff. He could smell his favourite smell. He sniffed and sniffed until he came to the smallest present with the big yellow bow. On the front in black letters was the message: Clovis Kitten, Happy Christmas.

Clovis knew the present was for him. He tugged at the ribbon and pulled at the paper until the present opened and out rolled his favourite chocolates.

"What a wonderful Christmas," thought Clovis as he finished his chocolates and licked his paws and curled into the corner of the best armchair.